Other books about Kevin and Katie

Katie Discovers Summer
Katie Discovers Winter
Katie Helps Mom
Katie Moves
Kevin and Katie
Kevin Discovers Autumn
Kevin Discovers Spring
Kevin Goes to School

First published in Belgium and Holland by Clavis Uitgeverij, Hasselt – Amsterdam, 2008
Copyright © 2008, Clavis Uitgeverij

English translation from the Dutch by Clavis Publishing Inc. New York
Copyright © 2010 for the English language edition: Clavis Publishing Inc. New York

Visit us on the web at www.clavisbooks.com

Kevin Helps Dad written and illustrated by Liesbet Slegers
Original title: *Karel helpt papa*
Translated from the Dutch by Clavis Publishing

ISBN 978-1-60537-065-1

This book was printed in january 2010 at Hung Hing Printing (China) Co., Ltd
in Hung Hing Industrial Park, Fu Yong Town, Shenzhen, 518103 China

First Edition
10 9 8 7 6 5 4 3 2 1

Clavis Publishing supports the First Amendment and celebrates the right to read

Kevin Helps Dad

Liesbet Slegers

Clavis

NEW YORK

"Good morning, Kevin."
Dad wakes me up.
I open my eyes and hear the birds singing outside. Today is going to be a great day.

Dad has a day off today. The two of us are going to do fun things. After breakfast, we put on our work clothes.

In the garage, Dad hangs clothes hooks on the wall. First, he makes holes with the drill. What a noise!

I have a toolbox just like Dad.
It contains pliers, screws, a
hammer and many other things.
With my tools, I can help Dad.

With my hammer, I hit the wall a bit to check if it's still strong enough. "Well, Kevin?" Dad asks. "Is the wall still all right?" Then he screws the hooks in.

The car is dirty. We wash it outside. With my sponge, I get everything wet. I can wash the bumper and the lights.

The inside of the car must be cleaned, too. I can sit behind the wheel. Now I am Dad! I imagine I'm driving to the store and honk, just like Dad does sometimes ...

The car is all shiny again. In the garage, we take off our wet clothes. Quickly, we put on something dry, and then I can go and play for a while.

In my toy chest is my teddy bear. Where are my books? Hey, look over here, my drum! Grandma gave it to me for my birthday.

Boom, boom, boom ... Yippee, Dad joins in! He takes the rattle and the bells. Together, we make great loud music.

"That was fun," Dad says. "But now it is time to make dinner, because Mom will be home soon. I will peel the potatoes. Can you wash them, Kevin?"

"Hi Mom! Look, Dad and I have made French fries!" "Yummy, that smells great," Mom inhales. "Give me a hug, my two sweet boys ..."